Mandy, Sam and Eddy's mum, died in January 1988.
The boys, with their dad, Adrian, helped to make
this special book in her memory.

First paperback edition 1996

Reprinted 1997

First published 1991 in hardback by
A & C Black (Publishers) Limited,
35 Bedford Row, London WC1R 4JH

ISBN 0–7136–4432–X

Text copyright © 1996, 1991 Ginny Perkins
Photographs copyright © 1996, 1991 Leon Morris

A CIP catalogue record for this book
is available from the British Library.

Filmset by August Filmsetting, Haydrock, St Helens
Printed in Belgium by Proost International Book Production

Remembering Mum

Ginny Perkins and Leon Morris

A & C Black · London

Sam and Eddy are in their back garden looking at the daffodils.

'They don't smell much, Eddy,' Sam tells his brother, 'but look how velvety this petal is. Do you remember when we planted these with Mum? You were only little then, but I can remember it really well.'

2

Dad comes and tells them it's time to go to school,
so Sam and Eddy get in the car.

The boys have another garden at school. It's in memory of their mum, Mandy, who died a little while ago. Soon after Mandy died, the boy's teacher asked their dad which were Mandy's favourite flowers. They decided to grow some for her in the playground.

The children went to the garden centre to choose some flowers, and planted them specially for Mandy. Sam and Ed like to have this special place to go and sit quietly and think about their mum. They look after it carefully too.

Watering Mandy's plants makes Sam feel sad. His best friend Paul gives him a hug. After Mandy died, Paul was always ready for a hug – that's what special friends are for.

As usual, Sam is cheered up by the bold
bare bear in his favourite book.

7

Sam's mum and dad found this twisted wood and the cone

Ed likes stories too – he decides to listen to a story tape. Sam does some writing about his mum and dad. They found this piece of twisted wood in the New Forest. That was before they had him or Eddy!

Sometimes Sam feels really sad when he thinks about his mum. But today he feels happy, just remembering how beautiful she was.

Ed thinks there's just time to do some painting before lunch. But he only has time to start.

'Ummm! Honey sandwiches for lunch,' says Sam, 'All that work's made me hungry.'

After lunch it's playtime, so Ed goes out to swing on the bars with his friends.

In the afternoon, Dad arrives early to pick up the boys. Ed explains that Dad will have to wait until they've finished what they're doing.

'We're making a model of our house for Mum's grave,' he says, 'and I'm helping to mix the colours.'

Sam wishes his mum was at home still. He remembers how she always loved whatever they made for her. He feels angry that he can't show her his little house.

As they walk to the flower shop, Eddy and Sam tell their dad about all the things that happened at school today. Sam carries the model, so Eddy says he wants to choose the flowers.

They always bring flowers when they visit their mother's grave. There are so many beautiful colours, it's hard for them to decide which ones to buy.

'I'll get daffodils,' says Ed. 'You buy freesias, Dad, Mum liked them best. The smell lasts longer but my daffodils are brighter. I know Mum would have loved them.'

Mandy is buried in a cemetery not far from their home. Sam and Eddy usually decide where to put the flowers they've brought her.

'Here, Dad,' Sam says. 'They will look good behind her name, and the wind won't knock them over.'

Adrian made the headstone from some old oak. It has Mandy's name on, and two days the family like to remember – Mandy's birthday and the day she died. This headstone isn't going to be there for long. The family want something really special for Mandy, so they are going to make a beautiful headstone out of marble.

This is when they all need a cuddle. Each of them
feels sad at Mandy's grave, but being close helps.
It's hard to think about anything except Mandy
when they're here together. That makes this place
very special.

'I know it hurts, boys,' Dad says, 'but we have
each other and we'll always have Mandy in our
hearts.'

Dad usually has a little cry at Mandy's grave.
So do Sam and Eddy. Sometimes their heads are
full of memories.

Carefully Sam puts his model house next to the
grave, then it's time to go home.

Back home there's lots to do and less time to think about Mum. After a quick scoot round the garden, Eddy goes inside to help Dad in the kitchen.

'Look, Dad, I'm doing this really carefully,' Eddy says, slowly opening a tin. They all love spaghetti dinosaurs for dinner.

'Dinosaurs and vegeburgers for dinner!' says Ed cheerfully, 'Watch me clean my plate!'

After tea, everybody has a job to do. Dad washes up while Sam keeps him company on Mandy's old recorder. Ed goes into the sitting room to sort out some old photographs and to bring out the photograph albums.

Before bed, Sam and Eddy and their Dad have a peaceful time, when they look together at photographs of the family.

Sam points at one. 'That's not me,' he says, 'I was never that tiny!'

Sam likes it when Dad leans his head against him. It makes him feel good. Eddy sees a picture of his dad cuddling his mum. He thinks it makes his dad feel sad – she looks so beautiful.

Time to get ready for bed. Ed stares in the mirror while he cleans his teeth.

'Remember what Mum taught us, brush round and round in tiny circles,' says Sam. But Sam's mouth is full of toothpaste, so Ed doesn't hear him.

At bedtime, Dad reads them a story.

Mandy's death has brought a lot of sadness to her family. It makes all of them try even harder to look after each other and be extra loving. Bedtime is often a special time for doing this. They feel really close ending the day together remembering Mum.